Streamline Graded Readers
Level 2

Y0-DDP-647

The Eyes of Montezuma

Stephen Rabley

Series Editors:
Bernard Hartley and Peter Viney

OXFORD UNIVERSITY PRESS
1988

Oxford University Press
Walton Street, Oxford OX2 6DP

Oxford New York Toronto
Delhi Bombay Calcutta Madras Karachi
Petaling Jaya Singapore Hong Kong Tokyo
Nairobi Dar es Salaam Cape Town
Melbourne Auckland
and associated companies in
Beirut Berlin Ibadan Nicosia

OXFORD is a trade mark of Oxford University Press

ISBN 0 19 421907 0

© Oxford University Press 1988

Illustrated by: RDH Artists

Printed in Great Britain by Thomson Litho Ltd, East Kilbride, Scotland

THE AMERICAN GIRL

Nick Harman stood at the back of the ship and watched England slowly disappear. 'That was a really wonderful holiday,' he said quietly.

His wife, Clare, smiled. 'Two weeks of rain in Cornwall and you thought it was wonderful?!'

Nick put an arm round her and laughed. 'Well, OK, the weather was bad, but you can't have an English August without rain.' He looked at his watch. 'When do we get to Santander?'

'Not until six o'clock this evening,' answered Clare. 'Then it's another four hours in the car to Madrid. It's going to be a long day.'

Nick looked down at the white water below them. 'It's also the last day of our holiday,' he said.

Suddenly he felt Clare's hand on his arm. 'Look,' she said and pointed to an old man on the other side of the ship. He was sitting in a red chair and reading a Spanish newspaper.

'What is it?' asked Nick.

'The Countess of Montalban has died,' replied Clare. 'It's on the front page of that man's newspaper. Isn't her grandson, José Duero, one of your students?'

Just then the old man stood up and put the newspaper under his arm. Quickly Nick walked across to him.

'Excuse me,' he said in Spanish. 'Could I borrow your newspaper for a few minutes?'

The man smiled. 'Yes, you can keep it, young man. But are you sure you want it? It's ten days old.'

'Yes, I'm sure,' said Nick. 'Thanks.'

Five minutes later Nick and Clare were sitting in one of the ship's lounges. There were two cups of coffee and the Spanish newspaper on the table in front of them.

'She was ninety-four,' said Clare.

'Yes,' replied Nick. 'She was also one of the richest women in Spain. José told me once about a pair of her earrings. What did he call them? Oh yes – the Eyes of Montezuma – that was it.'

'The Eyes of Montezuma,' repeated Clare softly.

Nick looked up from the newspaper. 'Hmm, the two biggest diamonds in Spain. They came from Mexico about two hundred years ago and have been in the family since then.' He turned the page. 'Well, until now,' he continued quietly. 'It says here "The Countess has given her famous earrings, the Eyes of Montezuma, to the Prado Museum in Madrid." Look . . . there's a photo.'

Clare put down her coffee cup and looked. In a glass case there were two very beautiful diamonds. It was only a black and white photo, but the diamonds shone like cold, white fires.

'The Eyes of Montezuma,' she repeated slowly. 'What a wonderful name.'

'Excuse me, could I sit at your table? All the others are full.'

Nick and Clare both looked up. There in front of them was a girl of eighteen or nineteen. She was pretty with short, dark hair and bright eyes.

'Yes . . . please do,' said Clare, and took her bag off the chair beside her.

'Thanks,' said the girl. She put a glass of milk on the table and sat down. 'Hi, I'm Shelley . . . Shelley Marn.' Her voice was American and she was wearing a T-shirt with a picture of James Dean on the front.

'Hello,' said Nick. 'I'm Nick Harman and this is my wife, Clare.'

The girl smiled at both of them, then pointed at the

newspaper on the table. 'Please, don't let me . . .'

'No, that's OK, we've finished,' said Clare.

The three travellers began talking. First, Nick and Clare told Shelley about their home in Madrid and their jobs. 'Nick's an English teacher and I work in a hospital,' said Clare. 'We've lived in Spain for almost two years now.'

Then Shelley told them about her life in the United States. She was a student at the University of California and lived in Los Angeles. 'This is my first time in Europe without my parents,' she said with a small smile. 'My family has friends in Zaragoza and I'm going to stay with them for a month.'

After about twenty minutes, Clare said, 'Would you like to stay and have lunch with us?'

'OK,' Shelley said. 'Thanks . . . thanks a lot. But first I must get my bag. I left it in the car.' She laughed. 'I have this little yellow Fiat. I bought it in England. And do you know why I chose it? I'm STM – Shelley Theresa Marn – and the letters on the car are STM, too!' She laughed again and stood up. 'Two minutes, OK?' Then she turned and walked out of the lounge.

But Shelley Marn didn't come back after two minutes, or ten, or twenty. Nick and Clare waited, but in the end they had lunch without her.

'I don't understand it,' said Nick when they left the restaurant.

'Neither do I,' replied Clare. 'She was so friendly.'

Several hours later they arrived at Santander in the north of Spain. It was early in the evening, but still very hot. In their car, the Harmans were waiting to leave the ship and begin the road journey to Madrid.

Suddenly Nick said, 'That's strange.'

'What's strange?' replied Clare.

'That Fiat,' Nick answered. 'The yellow one, two cars behind us. Didn't Shelley say her car was a yellow Fiat?'

Clare turned and looked. 'E754 STM,' she said quietly. 'It *is* her car.' Then she noticed the driver. It wasn't Shelley Marn. It was a big, dark-haired man wearing sunglasses.

A VILLA NEAR TOLEDO

Two days later in the Harmans' Madrid flat, Clare turned on the radio while she was making breakfast. 'Hurry up!' she shouted to Nick in the bedroom. 'We're going to be late.'

'OK, OK, I know . . . but I can't find my shoes,' replied Nick's voice.

Clare smiled. 'There's always something,' she thought.

Just then the radio news began. At first Clare didn't listen very carefully, but suddenly . . .

'Last night two of Spain's most famous and expensive diamonds disappeared from the Prado Museum. The diamonds – the Eyes of Montezuma – were in a special glass case on the museum's second floor. Police have begun . . .'

Nick walked into the kitchen with a pair of shoes in one hand. 'I've found them,' he said. Then he saw Clare's face and stopped. She was pointing at the radio. 'What is it?' he asked.

'Someone's stolen the Eyes of Montezuma,' Clare replied quietly. 'Listen.'

'. . . only ten days ago,' the voice on the radio continued. 'Before that they were in the Montalban family for two hundred years. And now the sports news . . .'

Clare got up and turned off the radio. 'When did it happen?' asked Nick. He sat down and put on his shoes.

'Last night,' Clare answered. 'Strange, isn't it? We were talking about them only two days ago on the ship. Now . . .'

Nick looked at his watch. 'Oh no, we really *are* going to be late. Come on, you can tell me the story in the car.'

The Countess of Montalban's eighteen-year-old grandson, José Duero, was one of Nick's students that morning. After

8

the lesson Nick said, 'I heard about your grandmother's diamonds, José. It's terrible. Have you had any news?'

José looked at his hands sadly. 'No, not a word, Mr Harman,' he said. 'They've gone, and we're never going to see them again . . . I'm sure of it.' He lifted his face and looked at Nick. 'You know,' he continued, 'my grandmother really loved the Eyes of Montezuma. Only a month ago she told me, "One day I want to give them to the people of Spain".' He stopped for a second and looked down again. 'That was the last time I saw her alive.'

Later that afternoon Nick had to give a lesson outside Madrid. On the way back he stopped because he needed some petrol. While he was waiting to pay, a man came out of the supermarket across the street. He was tall, fat and had dark hair. 'Where have I seen him before?' thought Nick. 'A student? No. Did he work at the hospital with Clare? No.' At that moment the man looked up at the sky, then put on a pair of sunglasses. Suddenly Nick remembered. 'You were the one behind the wheel of Shelley Marn's car!' he thought. Yes, he was sure of it. Quickly he paid and walked outside.

Just then a blue Renault stopped a few metres in front of the dark-haired stranger. The door opened and a woman's voice called, in English, 'Don't just stand there, you fool. Let's go.' The car began to move, and then Nick saw something. On the back seat there was a bag with the letters U.C.L.A. on the side. The University of California in Los Angeles . . . Shelley's university.

'I don't like this,' thought Nick. 'I don't like this at all.' He began to walk towards a telephone box, but stopped. No, there wasn't time to call the police. He turned, ran back to his car and started the engine. There was only one answer. He had to follow the blue Renault.

Nick's journey ended one hour later on a quiet country road near Toledo. The blue Renault stopped in front of a pair of heavy metal gates. There was a high wall on both sides of them, and a sign on the gates said 'KEEP OUT'. Quickly Nick stopped, too, and turned off his engine. He was two hundred metres behind the other car, but he could see everything. After a few seconds the gates slowly opened, the Renault drove inside, then the gates closed again. Nick looked at the 'KEEP OUT' sign. Now what? Back to Madrid? Call the police? 'No,' he said softly. 'Not yet.'

He got out of the car and walked towards the metal gates.

Through them, in the gold evening light, he could see an old, dark villa. It looked empty. Then he noticed a small building made of wood in the villa's garden. It had a big lock on the door and several broken windows. He could see something through one of them. Was it a small square of yellow? Yes, it was.

Carefully he climbed the wall and jumped into the garden. Inside he stopped, looked left and right, then ran quickly towards the small building. There he stopped again. The only

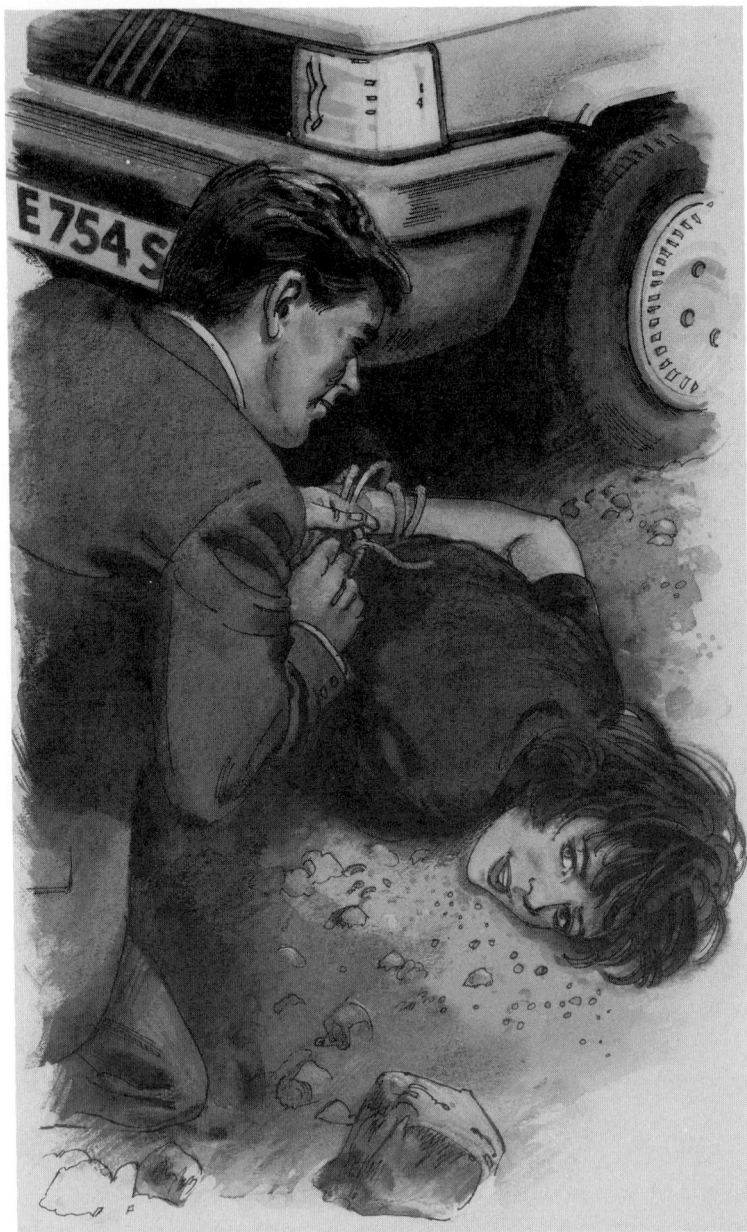

sound he could hear was the wind in the trees. Then, very slowly, he lifted his head and looked through one of the broken windows. Inside he saw the yellow Fiat and, on the ground next to it, Shelley Marn. There were ropes round her hands, feet and mouth.

Quickly Nick found a heavy rock and broke the lock on the door. Then he went inside and, with some glass from one of the broken windows, began to cut the American girl free.

'Oh, I am *very* happy to see you,' she said a minute later. 'But how . . . ?'

'That's not important,' said Nick. He began to cut the last rope round her feet. 'Tell me quickly. What happened on the ship?'

'Well,' said Shelley. 'I was getting my bag from the car when I heard voices . . . English voices. They were talking about a museum. Then one of them said something about stealing "the eyes".'

'The Eyes!' repeated Nick, and put down the piece of glass for a second. 'Now I understand.'

'That's when they noticed me,' Shelley continued. 'Then everything happened really quickly. A big man in sunglasses suddenly appeared. He had a gun and pointed it at me and said, "She's heard too much. We can't let her go." After that someone hit me from behind and everything went black. Then I woke up here.' She closed her eyes. 'It's all like a bad dream.'

'Well, don't worry. It's nearly over,' said Nick, and cut the last rope. 'There. Can you stand up? OK, we're going to . . .'

'You're not going to do anything,' said a man's voice. Nick and Shelley turned. In the open door there was a tall, dark shadow against the evening sky. It was the driver of the Renault and he had a gun in his hand.

THE PLANE TO MOROCCO

'Put your hands in the air and don't try anything clever!' shouted the man. Slowly Nick and Shelley put their hands in the air. 'Very good,' said the man more quietly. His eyes were moving quickly from side to side. 'Now turn towards the wall.' They turned.

Just then Shelley looked down. On the floor in front of her there was a rock . . . Nick used it a few minutes earlier when he broke the lock on the door. 'Well, it's now or never,' she thought. Quickly she dropped to the floor, turned and threw the heavy rock at the man. It hit him on the side of the head.

'You dirty little . . . !' he began and pointed his gun at Shelley, but Nick was too fast for him. In a second he turned and pushed the man's arm as hard as he could against Shelley's car. Something metal hit the ground. Then Nick heard Shelley's voice. 'It's OK,' she shouted. 'I've got the gun.'

Immediately the dark-haired man stopped. He looked at the gun in Shelley's hand and said, 'No, no, pl . . . please don't shoot m . . . me.'

'That's better,' said Nick. He walked to the door, looked outside, then closed it. 'Now,' he continued, 'you're going to be a good boy and tell us about the Eyes of Montezuma. That's right, isn't it, Mr . . . ?'

'Blane. My name's Harry B . . . Blane,' said the man. 'What do you want to know?'

Nick smiled. 'Everything,' he said. 'But first, where are the diamonds?'

'I haven't g . . . got them,' said Blane. 'They're in . . . they're in the villa. Harris and Drake have got them.'

'Harris and Drake?' asked Shelley.

'Paul Harris and Janice Drake,' Blane replied. 'They stole the diamonds. I didn't do anything. Really! I just drove the car. Please, don't . . .'

At that moment Shelley put a hand on Nick's arm. 'Someone's watching us,' she said, and pointed towards one of the broken windows. Nick looked through it and saw a woman on the other side of the garden. She was standing outside the villa and had a pair of binoculars in her hands.

'You're right,' said Nick. 'Come on, we can't stay here.'

'What are you going to do?' asked Harry Blane.

Nick turned. 'That's a very good question,' he replied.

Just then there was a sudden noise . . . It was a car engine. Nick looked through the window again and saw the blue Renault. It was driving away.

'They're escaping!' he shouted.

'What! Without me?' said Blane. 'The dirty . . .!'

'Quick, Blane,' said Shelley. 'Where are they going? Tell us.' She pointed the gun at Blane's head. *Now!*'

Blane's face went completely white. 'OK, OK . . . They're going to a small airport about twenty kilometres from here.

They're taking the diamonds to Morocco on a plane at nine o'clock.'

Nick looked at his watch. It was ten past eight. 'Come on, Blane,' he said. 'We're going to follow them, and you can show us the way.'

Ten minutes later Nick was driving as fast as he could along the narrow Spanish country roads. In the back seat Shelley was still holding the gun. Blane was beside her with a rope round his hands. 'The airport's about two kilometres from here on the left,' he said.

Then suddenly there was a loud noise behind them. Shelley turned. 'Oh no,' she said. 'We've got trouble, Nick. It's the police.'

Nick didn't answer.

'Well, aren't you going to stop?' asked Shelley.

'No,' answered Nick. 'This is too important. We haven't got the time.'

Shelley looked behind her again. Now there was a blue light on top of the police car and one of the men inside was talking on a radio. After a few seconds she said, 'Is all this really

happening? I mean . . . I came to Europe for a rest and a holiday.'

Just then they turned a corner and Blane shouted, 'There it is!' In front of them was a big field. On one side of it there were several low, modern buildings. Next to one of them was the blue Renault and in the middle of the field was a small plane. It was already moving.

'They're going to escape,' said Shelley.

'Oh no they're not,' replied Nick. They were now driving across the field towards the plane. The police car was only a few metres behind them.

'I'm going to drive in front of the plane, OK?' said Nick.

Blane looked at Shelley. His face was grey. Neither of them replied at first, then Shelley said, 'Nick, are you sure that's a good . . . ?'

But it was already too late. The next moment the plane was almost on top of them. Shelley could see the pilot's eyes. Then in a second everything changed. The plane suddenly turned to the left, one of its wings hit the ground, and it crashed in a ball of orange fire.

At eleven o'clock the next day, Nick, Shelley, Clare and José Duero all arrived at the Prado Museum. Outside, several

newspaper, radio and television reporters were waiting for
them.

'How do you feel, Ms Marn?' asked one of them.

'Tired,' replied Shelley, with a slow smile.

'What happened after the plane crashed, Mr Harman? Can
you tell us?' asked another.

'Well,' said Nick, 'first, Shelley and I told the police our
story. Then two fire engines arrived. A few minutes after that,
one of the fire-fighters found the diamonds in the plane. That's
all, really.'

'Harris and Drake died in the crash,' the reporter continued,
'but what about Blane? What's going to happen to him?'

'I don't know,' answered Nick. 'That's a question for the
police. Now, please excuse us.'

Inside the museum José took Nick, Shelley and Clare to the
second floor. There he showed them the Eyes of Montezuma,
back in their glass case again. For a moment nobody spoke.
Then Shelley put her face next to the glass and said softly,
'They are . . . *beautiful!*'

After that, José said to the Harmans and Shelley, 'Come and
have lunch with me at one of the best restaurants in Madrid.'

'Thanks, José,' said Clare. Then she turned to Shelley. 'What
time are you leaving for Zaragoza? Have you got time for
lunch?'

'Sure,' said Shelley, and they all went out of the building
through a back door. Then she looked up at the hot, blue sky
and half closed her eyes. 'Oh, but my sunglasses are in the car,'
she said. 'Just let me go and get them, OK? Can you wait here
a minute?'

'Oh no,' replied Clare. She took Shelley's arm and laughed.
'This time, Nick and I are coming with you.'

Exercises

1 Read through the story quickly and find this information.

1 The place where the Eyes of Montezuma came from 200 years ago.
2 Nick's job in Madrid.
3 The American city where Shelley lives.
4 The country where Shelley bought her car.
5 Shelley's middle name.
6 The time of day when Nick and Clare arrived in Santander.
7 The age of José Duero.
8 The nearest city to the villa.
9 The number of people who stole the Eyes of Montezuma.
10 The time of the plane to Morocco.

2 Are these sentences true (√) or false (×)?

1 The story begins on the last day of Nick and Clare's holiday.
2 Shelley has never travelled to Europe alone before.
3 The Countess of Montalban's son is one of Nick's students.
4 The Countess died at the age of ninety-four.
5 The Prado Museum is in Toledo.
6 Harris, Drake and Blane all died in the plane crash.
7 Nick and Clare had wonderful weather on their holiday in Cornwall.
8 Shelley's family has friends in Zaragoza.
9 Blane showed Nick and Shelley the way to the small airport.
10 Nick and Clare are both English teachers.

3 Complete the spaces in these sentences.

1 This is my first time in Europe without my . . . . . .'
2 He was sitting in a red chair and reading a Spanish . . . .
3 They came from Mexico about two . . . . . years ago and have been in the family since then.
4 It was a big, dark-haired man wearing . . . .

21

5 'One day I want to give them to the people of . . . . . .

6 On the way back he stopped because he needed some . . . . . .

7 A sign on the gates said '. . . . . OUT'.

8 Quickly she dropped to the floor, turned, and threw the heavy . . . . . at the man.

9 'They're taking the . . . . . to Morocco on a plane at nine o'clock.'

10 The next moment the plane was almost on top of them. Shelley could see the . . . . . eyes.

4 Comprehension questions

1 How long were the Eyes of Montezuma in the Montalban family?

2 How did Nick and Clare first meet Shelley?

3 Where does Clare Harman work?

4 How long have Nick and Clare lived in Spain?

5 What did Shelley leave in her car on the ship to Santander?

6 Why did Shelley buy the yellow Fiat?

7 Why were Nick and Clare surprised when they saw Shelley's car at Santander?

8 Why did the Countess of Montalban give the Eyes of Montezuma to the Prado Museum?

9 Where did Nick see Harry Blane for the second time?

10 What did Nick see on the back seat of the Renault?

11 What do the letters U.C.L.A. mean?

12 At the petrol station, why didn't Nick call the police?

13 How did Nick break the lock on the small building in the villa's garden?

14 How did Nick cut the ropes round Shelley's hands, feet and mouth?

15 Why didn't Shelley have lunch with Nick and Clare on the ship?

16 How did Janice Drake see Nick and Shelley from the villa?

17 How did Nick stop the plane?

18 Who found the Eyes of Montezuma after the plane crash?

19 At the end of the story, what did José say to Nick, Clare and Shelley?

20 What did Shelley leave in her car outside the Prado Museum?

5 Discussion questions

1 Why were the diamonds called the Eyes of Montezuma?
2 How did the newspapers report Nick and Shelley's story?
3 What did Harry Blane tell the police after the plane crash?
4 Why did Blane help Nick and Shelley to find the small airport near Toledo?

Glossary

binoculars: special glasses you hold in your hands; binoculars help
   you see things a very long distance away
bright: giving out a lot of light; shining
Countess: a title of nobility for a woman; 'King' and 'Queen' are
   also titles of nobility
diamond: a very hard, bright, expensive jewel, without colour
earring: a piece of jewellery; you wear it on or through the ear
field: a piece of land in the country, for animals or for growing food
fire-fighter: a person whose job is to stop fires
in the end: finally, e.g. *I waited for a bus for two hours, but in the
   end I had to walk home.*
lounge: a room where you can sit comfortably
mouth: the part of the face that opens for eating and speaking
museum: a building where people can see old, beautiful and
   interesting things
newspaper: large pieces of printed paper with news, photographs,
   etc, that people buy every day (or every week)
parents: mother and father
remember: opposite of 'forget'; when you think about something
   from the past
repeat: say again
rock: a large stone
rope: very thick, strong string
shadow: a dark shape
still: continuing up to the present time, e.g. *I made the coffee an
   hour ago, but it's still hot.*
sunglasses: dark glasses that you wear in strong light
traveller: someone on a journey
university: a place where people can go to study when they have left
   school
villa: a house (often a holiday home in the country or by the sea)
wing: one of the long, flat pieces of metal on the side of a plane